Sunflowers   Girasoles

By / Por Gwendolyn Zepeda

Illustrated by / Ilustraciones de Alisha Gambino

Spanish translation by / Traducción al español de Gabriela Baeza Ventura

Piñata Books
Arte Público Press
Houston, Texas

Publication of *Sunflowers* is funded in part by grants from the city of Houston through the Houston Arts Alliance, the Clayton Fund, and the Exemplar Program, a program of Americans for the Arts in collaboration with the LarsonAllen Public Services Group, funded by the Ford Foundation. We are grateful for their support.

La publicación de *Girasoles* ha sido subvencionada en parte por la ciudad de Houston a través del Houston Arts Alliance, el Fondo Clayton y el Exemplar Program, un programa de Americans for the Arts en colaboración con el LarsonAllen Public Services Group, fundado por la Fundación Ford. Agradecemos su apoyo.

Piñata Books are full of surprises!
¡Piñata Books están llenos de sorpresas!

Piñata Books
An Imprint of Arte Público Press
University of Houston
4902 Gulf Fwy, Bldg 19, Rm 100
Houston, Texas 77204-2004

Zepeda, Gwendolyn.
    Sunflowers / by Gwendolyn Zepeda ; illustrations by Alisha Gambino ; Spanish translation, Gabriela Baeza Ventura = Girasoles / por Gwendolyn Zepeda ; ilustraciones de Alisha Gambino ; traducción al español de Gabriela Baeza Ventura.
      p. cm.
    Summary: After helping her grandfather plant squash, onions, carrots, cabbage and other vegetables that her mother uses in soups and salsas, seven-year-old Marisol plants sunflower seeds in her neighbors' yards, and weeks later, everyone gets to enjoy the fruits of Marisol's labor.
    ISBN 978-1-55885-267-9 (alk. paper)
    [1. Gardening—Fiction. 2. Grandfathers—Fiction. 3. Hispanic Americans—Fiction. 4. Spanish language materials—Bilingual.] I. Gambino, Alisha, ill. II. Ventura, Gabriela Baeza. III. Title. IV. Title: Girasoles.
    PZ73.Z363 2009
    [E]—dc22

2008034623
CIP

∞ The paper used in this publication meets the requirements of the American National Standard for Permanence of Paper for Printed Library Materials Z39.48-1984.

Printed in Hong Kong by Book Art Inc. / Paramount Printing Company Limited
May 2017–July 2017
9 8 7 6 5 4

For Liz Salinas.
—GZ

To my grandfather, may your garden be plentiful in the next life.
—AG

Para Liz Salinas.
—GZ

Para mi abuelo, que tu huerto sea abundante en tu próxima vida.
—AG

My name is Marisol. I'm seven years old. This spring, I helped my grandfather make a garden.

Me llamo Marisol. Tengo siete años. Esta primavera le ayudé a mi abuelito a hacer un huerto.

First we got the ground ready. We pulled out the old plants and weeds. Then we mixed up all the dirt to make it soft. That took a long time. When we were done, it was time to plant the seeds.

Primero preparamos la tierra. Sacamos las plantas viejas y la maleza. Después mezclamos toda la tierra para suavizarla. Eso nos tomó mucho tiempo. Cuando terminamos, sembramos las semillas.

Grandpa had a lot of seeds. Some of them came from the store. Some of them came from the plants we grew last year.

Abuelito tenía muchas semillas. Algunas venían de la tienda. Otras venían de las plantas que cultivamos el año pasado.

We planted squash, onions, carrots and cabbage. My mother uses those for soup.

We planted garlic, tomatoes, cilantro and chili peppers. My mother uses those to make a spicy salsa.

We planted mint. My grandmother likes to put mint in her tea.

We planted watermelons. Those are for me and my brother. We love to eat watermelons.

Sembramos calabazas, cebollas, zanahorias y repollo. Mi mamá los usa para preparar sopa.

Sembramos ajo, tomate, cilantro y jalapeños. Mi mamá los usa para hacer salsa picante.

Sembramos menta. A mi abuelita le gusta ponerle menta al té.

Sembramos sandías. Ésas son para mí y para mi hermano. Nos encanta comer sandía.

The last thing we planted was sunflowers. They're the first plants to come out of the ground. They grow very fast and very tall. When they're finished growing, they look like big black eyes with long yellow eyelashes. Grandpa says that seeing them makes him happy.

Lo último que sembramos fueron girasoles. Son las primeras plantas que brotan de la tierra. Crecen muy rápido y llegan a ser muy altos. Cuando terminan de crecer, parecen grandes ojos negros con largas pestañas amarillas. Abuelito dice que se alegra al verlos.

When the sunflowers dry, the black part turns into seeds. Grandpa likes to eat the seeds with salt. He gave me a little bag of the sunflower seeds. But I didn't eat them. Instead, I decided to plant them.

Cuando los girasoles se secan, la parte negra se transforma en semillas. A Abuelito le gusta comerlas con sal. Me dio una bolsita con semillas de girasol. Pero no me las comí. Decidí sembrarlas.

One day, while I was walking to school, I put one seed in the corner of Mrs. Sosa's yard. She lives across the street from us.

Next I put one seed in the corner of Mr. Binh's yard. He lives next to Mrs. Sosa.

I kept walking, and I put seeds in the corners of all the yards on the way to school. When I got to school, I still had three seeds left. So I planted them in the playground, all three in a row. And then I went to my classroom.

Un día, mientras caminaba a la escuela, sembré una de las semillas en la esquina del patio de la señora Sosa. Ella vive enfrente de nosotros.

Después sembré una en la esquina del patio del señor Binh. Él vive al lado de la señora Sosa.

Seguí caminando y sembré semillas en las esquinas de todos los patios en el camino a la escuela. Cuando llegué a la escuela, me quedaban tres semillas. Así es que las sembré en el patio, en una línea. Y luego entré a mi salón de clases.

After I got home from school that day, it rained. When the rain stopped, the sun came out. The next day, it rained again. I couldn't play outside, so I looked out the window at the corner of Mrs. Sosa's yard. I couldn't see anything growing yet.

Ese día cuando llegué a casa después de la escuela, llovió. Cuando dejó de llover, salió el sol. Al día siguiente llovió otra vez. No podía jugar afuera, pero miraba por la ventana hacia la esquina del patio de la señora Sosa. No podía ver si nada estaba creciendo.

More days passed. Some days it rained, some days it didn't. I went to school. I played with my brother. I ate the soup my mother made. My grandmother taught me to make tea. And I almost forgot all about the sunflowers I'd planted.
Until one day . . .

Pasaron más días. Algunos días llovió y otros no. Fui a la escuela. Jugué con mi hermano. Comí la sopa que preparó mi mamá. Mi abuelita me enseñó a preparar té. Y estuve a punto de olvidarme de los girasoles que había sembrado.
Hasta que un día . . .

It was Saturday, and the sun was out. I was playing in the front yard with my brother.

"Oh, my!" Mrs. Sosa cried out across the street.

We looked to see what the matter was. In the corner of her yard, there was a tall green stem with a big yellow sunflower on top.

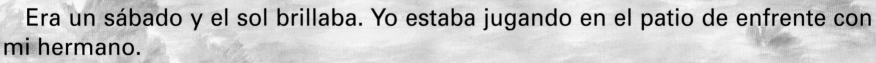

Era un sábado y el sol brillaba. Yo estaba jugando en el patio de enfrente con mi hermano.

—¡Válgame! —gritó la señora Sosa del otro lado de la calle.

Volteamos a ver por qué estaba gritando. En la esquina de su patio había un tallo alto con un gran girasol encima.

I took my brother down the street. Mr. Binh and all of our neighbors had sunflowers in their yards, too. We walked back to Mrs. Sosa's house and I told her about the seed I'd planted. I showed her where to get new seeds from the sunflower after it dried. I told her the seeds tasted good with salt. She said, "Thank you, Marisol."

I was happy she liked my surprise.

Caminé con mi hermano por la calle. El señor Binh y todos los vecinos también tenían girasoles en sus jardines. Regresamos a la casa de la señora Sosa y le conté de las semillas. Le enseñé de dónde sacar las semillas cuando el girasol se secara. Le dije que las semillas sabían rico con sal. Ella me dijo, —Gracias, Marisol.

Me alegró que le gustara mi sorpresa.

On Monday morning, I walked to school. There in the playground, I saw the three sunflowers I'd planted, standing tall all in a row. I showed them to my friends. I showed them to my teacher. I told them how to get the new seeds after the sunflowers dried.

"Thank you, Marisol!" my teacher said.

I was proud that I had taught my friends something new.

El lunes por la mañana caminé a la escuela. En el patio, vi los tres girasoles que había sembrado, todos paraditos en línea. Se los mostré a mis amigos. Se los mostré a mi maestra. Les expliqué cómo sacar semillas nuevas cuando los girasoles se secaran.

—¡Gracias, Mirasol! —me dijo mi maestra.

Estaba orgullosa de haberles enseñado algo nuevo a mis amigos.

That day, when I got home, I told Grandpa what I had done. He laughed, and I laughed, too. Then he asked me to help him in the garden again. It was time to plant pumpkin seeds, so that we would have pumpkins for Halloween.

Ese día, cuando llegué a casa, le dije a Abuelito lo que había hecho. Se rio, y yo también me reí. Después me pidió que le ayudara en el huerto otra vez. Ya era la época de sembrar las semillas de calabaza para que tuviéramos calabazas para el día de brujas.

I love gardening with Grandpa. When I grow up, I'm going to have my own garden. And the first thing I'm going to plant is sunflowers.

Me encanta trabajar en el huerto con Abuelito. Cuando sea grande, voy a tener mi propio huerto. Y lo primero que voy a sembrar son girasoles.

Gwendolyn Zepeda decided to become a writer in the 6th grade, because she liked to write long notes to her friends. In May of 2008, she published her first book for kids, *Level Up / Paso de nivel* (Piñata Books, 2012), *I Kick the Ball / Pateo el balón* (Piñata Books, 2011), *Growing Up with Tamales / Los tamales de Ana* (Piñata Books, 2008). So far, she has written three books for grown-ups. Gwendolyn has won awards for her writing, and sometimes you can read about her in newspapers and magazines. She likes to visit colleges and schools, where she reads her books out loud to students. Gwendolyn lives in Houston with her three sons and her pet cats. She is probably working on a new book right now.

Gwendolyn Zepeda decidió ser escritora en el sexto año porque le gustaba escribirles cartas a sus amigos. En mayo del 2008 publicó su primer libro infantil, *Level Up / Paso de nivel* (Piñata Books, 2012), *I Kick the Ball / Pateo el balón* (Piñata Books, 2011), *Growing Up with Tamales / Los tamales de Ana* (Piñata Books, 2008). Hasta ahora ha escrito tres libros para adultos. Gwendolyn ha ganado premios por sus obras, y a veces se puede leer de ella en periódicos y revistas. Le gusta visitar universidades y escuelas para leer sus libros a los estudiantes. Gwendolyn vive en Houston con sus tres hijos y varios gatos. Probablemente está escribiendo otro libro en este momento.

Alisha Gambino holds a Bachelor of Fine Arts in Illustration from the Kansas City Art Institute. Her influences are Frida Kahlo, Alphose Mucha, Diego Rivera and Hung Liu. She has completed and organized murals in the United States and Mexico. She has exhibited in many spaces such as Mattie Rhodes Art Gallery, Riverfront Gallery (Lawrence, KS), 3rd St. Gallery (Ozark, MO) and Art Expo New York. She has also illustrated for Rod Enterprises Cultural Graphics. Alisha teaches for Continuing Education at the Kansas City Art Institute and is the Art Education Curator for Mattie Rhodes Art Center.

Alisha Gambino se recibió con una licenciatura en Ilustración de Kansas City Art Institute. Entre sus influencias se encuentra el arte de Frida Kahlo, Alphose Mucha, Diego Rivera y Hung Liu. Ha organizado y completado murales en Estados Unidos y México. Ha expuesto sus obras en muchas galerías como Mattie Rhodes Art Gallery, Riverfront Gallery (Lawrence, KS), 3rd St. Gallery (Ozark, MO) y Art Expo New York. También ha creado ilustraciones para Rod Enterprises Cultural Graphics. Alisha es maestra de Continuing Education en Kansas City Art Institute y se encarga del arte educativo para Mattie Rhodes Art Center.